## ACKNOWLEDGEMENTS

Acknowledgements are due to the editors of the following publications in which some of these poems, or versions of them, first appeared: *North Yorkshire One Nine Nine* and *Teesway One Nine Nine* (Shutter Books), *The Intelligent Woman's Guide* and *The Grist Anthology of New Writing* (Bluetouch Publications and Grist Books in association with The University of Huddersfield), *Pearl Magazine, Taste* and *...Therefore I Am* (clan-u press, The University of Central Lancashire).

## BY THE SAME AUTHOR

*Dr James Graham's Celestial Bed (Comma 2006)*

First published in Great Britain in 2013 by Comma Press
www.commapress.co.uk

ISBN: 1905583273
EAN: 978-1905583270

**LOTTERY FUNDED**

The publishers gratefully acknowledge assistance from the Arts Council England North West, as well as the support of Literature Northwest:
www.literaturenorthwest.co.uk

Set in Bembo by David Eckersall
Printed and bound in England by Berforts Information Press Ltd

# Lifting the Piano with One Hand

GAIA HOLMES

# Contents

## LIFTING THE PIANO WITH ONE HAND

# DELFT AND DOULTON

**Blessed**

Your grandmother
had tins full of prayer tags
and soft Garibaldi biscuits.
She stored gossip like hymn sheets
folded into the back
of her breeze-block Bible,
kept a row of icons
above her fireplace
with garish hearts
like rotting plums,
reserved the best bone china
for priests, saints
and other visitations.

If you were lucky, upon leaving
you'd be blessed with a dry kiss
pressed upon the brow,
otherwise you'd leave
drenched in a frenzy of spittle,
Hail Marys and Holy Water.

You said I'd done *quite* well,
made a good impression
but I could tell by the way
she edged her way
around my name
and how damp I was
when we said goodbye
that she thought
I'd burn in Hell.

## Inland

And it comes to me
as we drive through moors
clotted with burnt, black heather,
where the air smells of sulphur
and scorched sugar.

Inland, away from you
the sky is a finger painting,
stale streaks of dark clouds daubed
above the slated roof tops.

You have to learn to register these things,
the sweet and the sour
moments of life,
each dead pheasant you pass
fluttering like a ball gown
in the motorway breeze,
each blurred wasp you see
pulped against the windscreen,
the frail mortality of colour.

Remember – this is the way you breathe,
like a symphony of echo
trapped inside a shell.

On days like this
there are certain things that you recall;
the clinging breeze loaded with salt,
dead fish rotting on the tide line,
the way that the edges of the land
blur and spread
and sink into the sea.

Remember that day when we woke
because the sun beams nudged us
out of our sticky nest of sloth.
Our ambition became sobriety.
We binned empty wine bottles
and sour milk,
scoured lust off the dishes,
sat out in the garden,
and waited for our hearts to dry.

## Ice Hotel

We have here
our own cheap little room
in the ice hotel
with none of the glamour
of a honeymoon bed.

We sleep on glaciers
with thick sheets of glass
between us.

Already
you have forgotten me.
My name turns blue
on your lips.

At night
the hotel glows
with its chandeliers
of seal-fat candles
and from the outside
you can see us,
you can see through us.
You can see
our meaty hearts
choking
under traceries
of frost.

## Retraction

Our sadness lives
on different floors,
separated
by a flimsy wafer
of carpet and board.

Mine is the feisty kind
that screams,
yours is the quiet rat
that gnaws.

Sometimes they meet
at the breakfast table,
spill milk, make chaos,
leave meaning out to sour.

But *we*
keep missing each other.
A fast car shrieks,
a bass-beat
jellies the house
or a cat keens and mewls
over our pleas
and we hear nothing,
only the tense creak
of our parallel pacing,
the gush and scratch
of something
scrubbing itself raw.

## Banshees

He heard the Banshees singing
weeks before she died.
Each night their cold blue keening
stained his dreams, or in the day time
one of their discordant notes
would find him, get lodged in his body
like a wasp trapped somewhere
between his heart and his brain.

I tried to diffuse their mournful racket,
trained myself to coo like a wood pigeon,
to breathe like yeast expanding in proving dough,
to whisper like the soft crackle of crocus shoots
pushing through the crust of a bulb.
I asked the wind to sing something gentle,
told the moon to hum as it nosed its way
through the dark, worked hard to raise
the volume of our bodies as we loved:
our hearts thumping, our blood roaring,
our bones colliding.

But on that day I had no song strong enough
to hold them back.
They came wailing, whey-faced, raw-eyed,
stood at the end of the bed and sang him
the long demented opera
of her death.

**All I Can Do for You is Dream...**

I know you'll be awake now.
You'll be out in the garden shed
as far away as you can get
from the house and its damp wreaths,
its stink of grief and lilies.
You'll be sitting amongst
plant pots, pegs and windfall apples,
smoking cigarettes.

Here the street is sleeping.
I skulk around the kitchen
in the dull fridge light, avert my eyes
and tiptoe past the pink sloe gin.

I could drink now.
I could drink for me, for you,
for the whole of the island.
I could drink for remembrance,
knock back a teacup for all the dead souls
searching for that bright crack back into life.
I could drink now but it's 4am
and I've got an empty bed to fill
and dreams to dream for both of us.

**Occasional China**

This morning
I packed away
my black suit,
dressed
in something pale,
sat in the outhouse
and scraped the grief
off my boots,
caught the train
and tried to forget
the sound
of occasional China
rattling
in trembling hands.

## Cillit Bang

*'Let's not kid ourselves. There's no magic solution to cleaning your surfaces. Many of today's cleaners simply don't perform, particularly on tough stains like baked-on grease, bathroom grime, soap scum and lime scale. With all the scrubbing required, they leave you doing most of the hard work. Before you give up, try Cillit Bang! Its revolutionary, powerful cleaning formula amazingly removes even the toughest stains and dirt right before your eyes. You need to see it to believe it. Try Cillit Bang: Bang, and the dirt is gone!'*
*— cillitbang.co.uk*

All those ghosts that have been haunting me,
all those boggarts, dead dogs and mad men,
I blasted them with Cillit Bang
and they slowly disappeared
leaving no smudges, smears or greasy stains,
leaving clean reflections of the sky
on every surface.

Cillit Bang can cut through the grime
that our lives have become caked in,
take us back to those lusty, lucid days
when your clear gaze and my bright teeth shone.
It can turn our bruises into tiger's eyes and opals,
gloss our scummy hearts and make them gleam
like polished brass.

I've been in control of my life
since I discovered Cillit Bang.

Emotional salvation is no longer a chore:
one blast quickly licks away the stains
left on the pale parts of our souls.
*Bang, and the dirt is gone.*

And when those heavy words
begin to fall from your mouth,
those words I don't want to hear,
I spray them with Cillit Bang
before they have time to settle,
before they have time to sink in.

## Dry

Our whole loving kingdom
is crumbling.
Ornamental hearts
have fallen off gateposts.
The sun-sucked river
is hissing for alms.

There were words once.
Now they're gone,
wiped off your lips
like biscuit crumbs
and I have nothing,
just the dry silence,
the murmur
of things dissolving.

The birds' dawn chorus
has brittled,
it drops to the floor
like October leaves
and I sit here
trying to tap the void,
trying to remember a life
pumped full of colour:
nights tinged
with peacock green
or cold blue canticles of frost,
trying to remember
the time when
you wove meaning
into my name.

I know that
salvation will come
with the thunder,
the parched banks of the river
will slacken and swell,
your crisp touch will soften
in the kindness of rain.
Our thin tongues
will fatten with song.
And, ignited by lightning,
our eyes
will flash fever again.

## Closed

My kitchen
is crawling
with little Christs.

There are
broken prayers
all over the carpet
and the house
smells of lethargy
and turnips,
sags with the weight
of hopeless vowels.

Somewhere
across the scuff
of heather, hair pin bends
and the gloss of tar and roadkill,
you sit in a pub
with the sea slandering me
at your elbow

and though there is one of my hairs
tangled around the button
on your cuff,
you do not think of me.
Your open palm
curls in,
retracts
like a dead spider
and the question
is closed.

# The AA Road Atlas of Britain

The battered road map
was your Bible.
Whenever you spread
its well-thumbed landscapes
across the duvet
I became anxious,
the dog became anxious,
began to tremble
and pissed at the end of the bed.

Your palms were patterned
with curling country lanes.
Mine were cracked with worry
and split lifelines.

You kept moving,
walked in your sleep,
crossed oceans and deserts,
travelled light.
I was static,
flattening the mattress
with my hefty routines,
my bulging notebooks,
my useless plaster saints.

You used to study my body
like a cartographer,
reading the lines of my bones
like mysterious B roads,
working out
the best route

to my heart
but after a while
I became too familiar,
my name got rubbed away.
I became an unmarked town
with boarded-up windows
and spluttering neons.
No shops, no pubs, no petrol station
and only one demented resident
stinking of gin and loneliness
who kept the teapot warm,
ready to be filled
and the best bone china teacups
laid out on the table,
who waited for you to pass through
in your car full of firewood
and stories,
who waited for you everyday,
who tried to catch you,
who tried to beg you
to stay.

## Another Country

You have grown up now, grown out of me.
Grief has turned you into a different man;
someone who has no faith
in kindness or wishbones.

Stiff-necked, you drive us
across the border in your father's car,
talk us through a history of wounds,
take us to the petrol station
with its old fashioned pumps and oil cans.

You say it hasn't changed.
It still smells of sawdust and paraffin,
still sells the same soft biscuits
and cheap cigarettes.

We drive through Northern villages
where Christmas shouldn't be happening, but it is.
Tinselled fir trees sparkle through cottage windows.
Inflatable snowmen wobble on lawns
and this *is* another country, and home
is a gentle legend that holds no veiled mirrors,
no leaking lilies, no evidence of death.

Everything is distant here.
Sleep. Normality. You.
And more than ever I feel like a foreigner,
your clumsy little Sassenach stumbling
through the rosary, breaking teacups,
trying to grasp the etiquette of tragedy,
edging my way around your mother's kitchen
like a crab.

And I think that, to you now,
I have become another country,
a place you once lived in,
a life that you must leave behind.

**Jesus Feet**

I've wept on them, wished on them,
prayed on them so many times
but nothing's come of these little acts of faith
and I'm putting your skinny Jesus feet
in the top drawer of the freezer,
squeezing them in between the oven chips
and the frozen garden peas.

Elsewhere you are someone else's salvation
and you are working miracles.
You are driving her to important meetings.
You are baking stylish golden loaves of bread.
You are turning her bathwater into good red wine.
You are putting up shelves.
You are saying her name with meaning.


I'd be happy with half a miracle,
something close to a blessing,
a tender visitation
but I'm tired
of all these late night vigils
with the kettle ready to be boiled
and the tea bag ready in your cup
and our bed laundered, scented
and ready to be filled.

So I'm replacing my hope
with a lack of expectation.
I'm replacing
the Technicolor image of your face
with the faded, dog-eared poster
of an unimportant saint.

## House Clearance

Slowly she's clearing things out
starting with the useless items;
chipped china cups, trust
shot-through with hairline cracks,
orphaned plugs and fuse wire,
the dead stereos
he'd planned to resurrect.

And then there are the things
she'd like to keep
but knows she'll never use;
those bright, rich nights
that no longer fit,
the creaking songs
of the bed frame
now dull and flat
and out of key,
the sugared lovers' lingo
that has settled like cobwebs
in the corners of the room.

And love, what's left of it,
she boils up the bones,
flavours the vapid broth
with stock and spice,
sets up a soup shack
on the ragged edge of town
and serves it to the homeless,
the hungry, the loveless creatures
of the night.

## Punchline

I wanted to cheer you up
with a joke
but the chicken got mashed
by a truck
as it crossed the road,
the three psychiatrists
were blinded by exploding glass
as they tried to change
a light bulb
and the horse got coshed,
hung and carved into steaks
after ordering a beer
in the bar.

I wanted to cheer you up
with a joke
but my punchline
is all knuckle
and no flesh.
My punchline is
that I love you
and for once I tell you
in the right order
and at the right moment
but you are not amused.

# VISITATIONS

# Someone Should Tell her Mother she's Taking Drugs

I'm not a nosy neighbour, a curtain twitcher
but there are things you just can't help noticing.

She's one of *them*. You know the kind,
all joss sticks, earth mothers and mandalas,
all mung beans, patchouli and window-box herbs.

Each day there's a constant procession
of men and women, pimps and poets
knocking on her door.

She has lots of lovers.
One morning I saw a whole army leaving her house
glowing and glistening with post-coital sweat.

I'm not narrow minded.
I know that she's probably a nice young lady.
I think she's just mixing with the wrong crowd.

I've seen her dancing with the devil
through a crack in her curtains.
There they were, in her living room - naked.
Her- white as milk-top cream,
him- red as a pillar box, twisting and writhing,
their fingers turning into snakes.

Each month when the moon is full
her walls breathe. The bricks inhale and exhale.
The shrubs in her garden mumble maledictions.
Thick red light emanates from her letter box,
bleeds onto the street killing dandelions, scabbing in cracks.
Up in her attic she conducts a choir of split-tongued harpies.
They sing the Psalms backwards,
set car alarms screaming and town dogs barking.

She snorts cocaine, sleeps in a coffin,
eats dead kittens drowned in gin.
She keeps wolves in the cellar
and mermaids in the bath tub,
washes with absinthe and brimstone soap.

I'm not the type to make judgements.
I'm a liberal thinker.
I just worry about her welfare.
I think someone should tell her mother
that she's taking drugs.

It's girls like her
that give this street a bad name.

## Ghosts

I'm up late most nights,
drinking wine, talking to ghosts
who come to me with lullabies,
with vodka, with bruises.

Some leave buttons,
lucky scarabs and hair-pins.
Some leave brittle sprigs of heather,
half-smoked cigarettes,
a sticky band of rum
in the bottom of a glass.

Some leave postcards
from the places I never went
showing orange groves and vineyards,
winter village scenes
and rows of small, neat girls
with Michaelmas candles
in their eyes.

Sometimes when these ghosts
have gone the walls slacken,
the rooms expand,
and I feel a chill,
smell the tang of blood,
turn to see
your blue frost-caked hand
lolling from the wardrobe,
the raw slop of a still-born song
glistening on the carpet,
turning buttercups
into bell-shaped scabs.

## Remembrance

They ate nothing
all day
except for smoke,
desire,
the colours
dripping
from the sun.
Hunger
made her fingers
sharp and careless.
Her fevered touch
burnt its way
through skin
until
it hooked itself
around his backbone,
until
it probed its way
through sanctity
and brushed
against his soul.
Then it felt
as if someone
was walking
across
the unpacked dirt
above his grave.
It felt as if
someone had
remembered him.

## Smooth

He wants to show her off to his friends,
open her mouth and let them see
the solid curl of Kerrygold butter
that's not going to melt
on her chilled and temperate tongue.

He likes to believe
that the intellect she seems to lack
is fizzing somewhere deep in her subconscious
in a clever little room at the back of her brain
and comes out in Latin
when she sleeps.

He imagines that her fantasies
are of chocolate box babies,
pruning and marriage
but never of sex.

He wants parts of her
laser-printed onto his dinner plates,
wants to eat Spaghetti Bolognese off her face,
lick the gravy from the sills of her eyes,
suck the beef juice off her lips.

When he gets the chance
to get close enough
he will breathe her in.
Her sweat will smell
of caramel and roses.

# Rough

You were never a Nivea guy,
but often sat with your elbows
soaking on cut potatoes
or with green avocado pulp
buttering your face.

Smooth, you were,
unlike me with my clumsy tongue,
my Brillo pad hands
and my fish-knife finger nails.

You read the wilderness in me,
took note of the way
I could duck a wasp sting,
light fires with wet wood
and you tried to soften me,
imagined ironing out my voice,
dreamed me into chintzy parlours,
had me pouring tea
into fine bone china,
whispering to the aspidistra.

*Rough,* you used to say
when we were in bed
and my crusty heel
grazed your shin bone.
*Too rough.*

## The Guest

He smells of roast beef
and griddled pork chops,
has slack liver lips
and cold pudgy fingers
like uncooked chipolatas
ready for peeling fat, skin
and oily crackling.

The bed frame's brittle bird bones
strain beneath his bulk.
He leaves ragged wishbones
and slugs of red sauce
scabbing on the pillows,
makes the sheets stink of gravy,
stains the sides of the bath
with a tide line
of second-hand blood.

At night he thinks of her
basting in her delicate sweats,
dreams of sucking
her hot prawny toes
as he bakes in the darkness
of the guest room
and longs for her,
pale as boiled haddock
knotted into a filmy dressing gown
the colour of kidneys,
gnawing her nails
to the quick.

# The Man Who Dripped Digitalis

He could charm the poison out of foxgloves
and used his skills to quicken my pulse.
I wondered what he fed on, frayed liturgies
and the secret dreams of women,
toxic spores translated into messages
of lust, slivers of the dank March sky
rolled up like pickled herring.
I never knew. He always skimmed me,
left me hooked on some potent pollen,
some sacrificial line,
some cold gap between sentiments.

His fingers were like cathedrals,
too big to untie my delicate knots
yet he knew me inside out like he knew
the names of flowers and bats and clouds,
like he knew how to throw daggers
without skewering the soul.
He could sniff out creeping wolf-men
and crack their backbones with a lazy wink,
worked my fingers to his throat
like a snake charmer,
made me slide and arch with his singing breath.
After we'd loved and I was doped up on glow
he laid wet silver on my eyelids
believing it would bring him luck.

## The Glass House

Winter has sucked the landscape
back to black and white
but in the glass house
the world is plump and curved,
full of juice and spectrums.

We sit on the edge
of the vicious garden
where tropical flowers
shred the light with their teeth.
The steamy scent
of sap and green life
soaks through our coats
and makes us sweat.

In here, nothing is subtle.
Hungry proboscis leer
and lick the balmy air.
Colours pulse, drip and dazzle.
Petals do not drift or whisper,
they drop onto the dirt
with a succulent thud:
*He loves me, he loves me not.*

Later I will remember
the languid names of plants
that kill with sweetness;
*Nepenthes, Pinguicula, Saracenia.*
I will think of those gentle Latin nouns
turning into sensuous verbs
and I will think of him,
his shy soapstone fingers
turning into claws.

## Visitation

So this is it.
This is the night.
Downstairs the sofa
doesn't know me anymore,
my guest plates
are cracking with boredom,
the front door
is guarded by foxgloves
and throttled with toad-flax
and this is it. This is me,
mad woman in the attic
sifting the air for gold-dust,
a circle of crushed moths
patterning the carpet
around my feet,
cold coffee at my elbow,
logic in a hip-flask,
and I'm drinking wine
that tastes of hay
and Salamanca in July
and we're all waiting
for the storm, an answer,
a fag-burn in the sky,
words etched into the slick streets,
the soft porn of rain
on the skylight window.
We're all waiting
for our dead dogs
to rattle up the stairs,
we're all waiting
for our grandmothers
to polish our eyes
with spit

on the corner of a vest,
we're all waiting
for someone to say our name
with meaning.
We're all waiting,
ears angled cat-like,
waiting
for a car to pull up,
waiting
for inspiration
to open the door and enter
smelling of life,
of blood,
of little deaths,
of unspeakable notions
and say *I'm yours.*
*Take me now.*

## Murdering my Darlings

Following your advice
I have removed all excessive,
ornamental language from this poem.
The reader will no longer find
the small orgasmic palpitations
of hummingbirds' wings
in the seventh stanza
or cherry stones
spat out like rabbit hearts
in the second line.

I have also removed the scents
that permeated this verse,
the perfumes that you said
stank of clichés.
Now this poem smells
of the empty, anaesthetic void
of doctors' waiting rooms.
This poem reeks of service stations,
slack cement and indifference.

I have erased all references
to fruit, philosophers
and obscure alcoholic drinks
and replaced them
with more accessible imagery
such as broken bus shelters,
abandoned shopping trolleys,
dogs and mackintoshes.

You hinted that my poem 'tries too hard'.
You will be pleased to note
that this revised version
doesn't try at all.
I have also applied your wise advice
regarding structure
and altered all the line

breaks.

And though I trust and value
your suggestions,
though I know that
your constructive criticism
will make this a better poem
I'm afraid I have to leave the thin scientist
eating rice with a pair of tweezers
in the final verse.
I have to leave spilt wine, a broken topaz choker
and blood stains on the bed sheets.
I have to leave the old woman
who keeps the moon
in a bowl like a goldfish
radiating amber light across the page.

## Landscape

You will come wet-fingered
and blur my outlines,
smudge the neat shapes I've drawn
into the colours of the sky,
until angles and pencilled edges
become a wash, a mulch, a mess.

Let me draw us safely now.
Stick man, stick woman,
fingerless, faceless and stark
with a six mile gap between us
expressing nothing – toneless and bland
except for our fat magenta hearts.

**Wish**

Before, there is richness,
each one of their words
glowing on the sheets
like bonfire sparks,
the street lights
infusing the room
with a syrupy light

but afterwards
the night sucks back its magic,
the walls breed stains of shadow
and they lie together
tepid and dull as cold porridge
growing a skin of silence.

He gets up to let the mewling cat out,
leaves her, thin, grey and pathetic
as a birthday candle
that's been burnt and wished on
in the middle of his bed.

## Jig

There is
the smoke

and the scratch
and the jig

of bones
and the wheeze

of leaves
and the spark

in the eye
and the bellows

flaming
the flailing heart

and a magician stands
in my front room

bringing
my dead words
back to life.

## Quake

For months
I've been saving hope
in a blue pot-bellied jug.
But tonight I let it out
and it ran like a cat
that knows
it wants to kill
and crunch a skull
and feel a heartbeat
slowing
on its tongue.
Tonight I let it out
and there was silence,
a stiff, sucked-in stillness,
then the sound of
coat hangers cracking.
The dresses in my wardrobe
shimmied and fluttered
and stilled
like skewered butterflies
and the colours
that I had forgotten
were caught.

## Origami

Sometimes
you just have to remove yourself
from the landscape
before your lips
curl up and dry out
like ferns,
before your heart breaks down
and dissolves into the rain-sodden dirt,
before you stain the horizon
with your smile.
So I fold up my life
like origami,
squeeze it
into my pocket
where I slowly
disappear.

## House of Sticks

For him, mornings are thin as silk.
He drinks his coffee without milk or sugar,
loads his toast plate with wishbones,
writes long lists
of the things he cannot hold.

In the evening
he takes prayers instead of soup,
dines on the hum of the fridge,
the drip of the tap,
the hiss of the boiler pipes.

For him
the hills are too fat,
too sweet and green,
too loud and bloated with life.
He'd like to iron them out,
starch them
and hang them on his empty walls.
He'd like to understand them.

He'd like a house of sticks,
a bed of nails,
some pain
to rest his weight on.

## Home Sick

and what do you do
when you get the feeling
and you can't clamp it
between your finger tips
like a green fly,
hold it up to the light
and see it glow?
There's nothing
definite,
it's just a feeling,
a mulch of senses
and there's nothing
concrete,
you can't draw it,
you can't write it
and there's no door
sealing a place,
a memory you can
walk back into.
It's like the raspy kiss
of particular slippers
on linoleum,
like the switch
of a particular kettle
clicking as it boils,
like the glimmer
of a particular gilded
dog-eared poster
of Christ on a wall
in a place you might
or might not have lived.

It's an anxious
and displaced fragment
of something
somewhere
triggered by plaster
flaking like filo pastry
from the soft gable ceiling
when you punch it,
when you need
the simple ache
of bruises
rather than
the ambiguity
of words.

# LIFTING THE PIANO
# WITH ONE HAND

# I am Lifting the Piano with One Hand

I am holding it effortlessly steady
like a graceful waitress balancing a tray
of quail's eggs and salmon soufflé
on her horizontal palm.

I am dexterously carrying it up three flights of stairs
without stubbing my toes or splitting my fingernails,
without chipping paint off the door frames
or denting the soft plaster of the walls.

I am lifting the piano with one hand.
I have not eaten spinach, mineral supplements,
muscle powder or Weetabix.
Today I am just unusually strong
and able to carry the piano up three flights of stairs
where I'll leave the skylight window open
and a note inviting any passing ghosts
to come in, sit down and play 'Moonlight Sonata'
or 'Chopin's Nocturne' or 'The Entertainer'
or whatever they'd like to play on a neglected piano
in the house of a strong woman.

## Carnival Days

*For Vicky and Gary*
*08/08/08*

There will be carnival days
when the cat skits and tangos
and catches moths
and you're joyfully tangled
in paint and wire angels

and the kitchen table
is a magpie's feast of butterflies
and beads and things that shine
and he sings in German
as he washes up
and the kettle sings,
and the cooker sings,
and the wood pigeons sing,
and the potatoes
in their loamy beds sing
and the house hums
with a gutsy opera
of loving and living.

There will be quiet days
when laburnum lamps
glow in the six o'clock sun
and the bees whisper
as they tap honey
from the cores of flowers
and the cat purrs
in a svelte grey knot on the sofa
and you will sit together

reading books, trading lines,
sharing names, sharing
the subtle language
of contentment,
breathing in
the hushed glossolalia
of love.

## Swans

The days
are full of angles.
They strut
around the house
like vicious swans,
pecking
at piles of shoes
and clothes
and tangled thoughts,
hissing
at the disarray.

Smoothness
only comes
in the night
like a swallow
with the burr
and back-draft
of a wing,
with a memory,
with the swoop
of a hip-bone,
with the slow,
soft reel-show
of two cigarettes
thinning the gloom,
curing the darkness
with gold.

## Lallation

Those nights of inhabiting
someone else's stories
have been locked away.
Stained cotton sheets
have been folded
and stacked in storage.
Dog-eared sprigs
of browned silk flowers
have been binned.
She has developed a cleaner,
more sophisticated technique
that uses the shaping of the mouth,
the pressure of the tongue
pushed against the teeth,
the soft delivery
of exquisite plosives
and shimmering fricatives,
the whisper of affricates
or the richer, darker songs
of Os and Es and As
swooping from her lips
like pipistrelles,
so that where once
there were distended eyes
and needling fingers
there is just the calm burr
and cadence
of her breath,
the erotic lallation
of her song.

## I'd Like to Live in a French Film

where the thin tea-brown light
paints me wise and beautiful,
where the Sacre Coeur bells
and my neighbour playing Satie
make a stinging soundtrack
to my life.

Nothing will be bland:
you will be addicted
to my skin,
you will smoke
stumpy Gauloises cigarettes,
fill your car
with lust and violet clouds
as you drive through storms
dodging monstrous wind-fall trees
and toppled telegraph poles
just to get to me,
just to plant little kisses
like forget-me-nots
at the top of my thighs.

And in the morning,
every morning
we will drink black coffee
from shallow bowls,
we will eat croissants.
Our bed will become a table
full of love, books,
butter and crumbs
and outside

the wet streets will shine
like pewter,
the world will smell
of Montparnasse cafés
and Parisian rain.

## Cinematic Snow

This isn't matinee snow.
This stuff is mean and crusty.
It sticks in your throat
like goose down and cuttlebone.
It tricks you into slipping.

After five days
snowmen have morphed.
Hardened with a skin of ice,
their heads are frozen missiles,
their fat greying bellies
are wrecking-balls
that could crush a small cottage
or flatten a cat.

Matinee snow is gentle.
It shimmers on eyelashes.
It twinkles in beards
like chips of mica.
It is lovingly kissed
off lips and noses
and bluing fingertips.

Matinee snow inspires the thoughtful
to visit the needy
bearing steaming jugs of custard
and bowls of winter crumble
wrapped in tea-towels.

This isn't matinee snow.
It's the kind of snow
that makes the lonely even lonelier,
the kind of snow that will not soften

enemies or silence,
the kind of snow that makes you think
of cracks, knives and lies
and all the dangerous things
in the world.

## Back to Beige

You have to have lived a little
before you settle into a placid pastel life.
You have to have crossed the road
when the red man's glowing,
eaten Christmas cake in June,
sparked, burned and blown
before you bin your midnight dresses
and your winkle-picker boots.

You have to have died a little
before you know what it's like to shine,
gorged on colour before you settle for beige.
You have to have slept naked on a beach
wearing the moonlight as an eiderdown,
you have to have chosen love over money
and starved.

You have to have gone out for dinner
with your demons, dined on your vices
and mopped up the juices
with sin-eater's bread
before you put your life
into the hands of faultless angels,
before you let ambition
quietly pad out through the cat-flap,
before you give yourself over
to fate.

# I Turned my Heart into a 2-Star B&B

hoping that I might trick you
into checking in.
I covered the uneven walls
with red flock
and tawdry dados,
painted the ceiling
nicotine yellow,
hung dog-eared landscapes
at subtle slants,
put a back-lit tank
of Angel Fish in the foyer,
left stacks of browning
*Readers Digest*
on a pouffe in the lounge.

I transformed myself into a Mistress
of Marigold gloves
and tremulous ash cones,
wore pressed pin-curls
and a lilac housecoat.
And the only way you might
see through my disguise
would be when I slid your
grease-jewelled breakfast
onto the yellowed oil-cloth table,
bent low and close
so that my powdery cheek
dusted your jaw
and beneath the new
Jiff and liver scent
of my neck
you smelled wood smoke
and coconut
and remembered me.

## Matches

These years
I fill my days
with matchsticks,
build palaces
with balsa wood and glue,
go to sleep
with my virginal hand
stuck to the skin
above my heart.

I've built dance halls,
filled them with the sound
of her rustling skirts,
seasoned the floor
with cologne that smells
of the lily-of-the-valley
scent she used to wear.

I've built chapels
where we might have wed,
graveyards
where we might have been laid.
Our stiff dancers'
bodies pressed together,
our tulles and taffetas
folding and creasing
and fusing.

Her body
was wrapped in air,
my moth-fingered
hand cupped her elbow,
my palm

kissed her shoulder blade
too lightly to gauge the meaning
of her bones.

## Carmelo's

On Albion Street, squeezed between Pisces fishmongers
and Custace's game shop there is a little slice of Italy.
A tiny stereo plays Mina Mazzini's greatest hits
as Carmelo flours his rounds of soft calzone dough.
All day a gush of butchers' slop trickles past his shop,
a slurry of gills and gizzards and shreds of hide.
Carmelo grins above the gore, spins pale manna on his
fingertip:
'A calzone Madame? Nice with the coffee, the tea.'
But he says it like a tragedy, as if he's announcing a death.
No one stops. His beautiful cubes of feta run like milk
as the sun shines hard, turns pig's blood into clots
and the dead rabbits swinging beside his sign
begin to drip.

## The Operation

I anaesthetise you
with my brandied breath
and gently open
up your back
with a sharp
and loving knife.
For weeks
I've been in training,
my hands have drunk in
the stillness
of Lombardi lakes,
the secrets
of a watchmaker's calm
so I am very careful
not to touch your heart
as I disentangle
the knots of angst
that have formed
around your bones,
dislodge lost days
trapped like cold coins
between your ventricles
and unwind
congested cogs
of tension
until
they stop screaming
and begin to sing.
Afterwards
I weld the edges
of the gash together

with my burning thumb
and seal the wound
with dog oil.
When you wake
you remember nothing
except the thick
deep sleep,
the powdery sound
of the night dissolving
and the sensation
of soft wings
skimming your veins
but you feel different,
refreshed,
as if you've stepped
out of a life of angles
and into a world of curves.

## Brie

'The in-depth Cheese & Dreams study, a first of its kind, reveals that eating cheese before bed will not only aid a good night's sleep but different cheeses will in fact cause different types of dreams... What is particularly interesting is the reported effect different types of British cheese have on influencing the content of dreams. It seems that selecting the type of cheese you eat before bedtime may help determine the very nature of often colourful and vivid cheese-induced dreams...'

After she left
he consoled himself
by eating pickled onions in bed
and sleeping in his socks
but after a while
his nights began to reek.
Vinegar seeped into his dreams.

He dreamed of derelict kitchens
with cupboards full of hearts in jars,
black, lonely and bitter
as pickled walnuts.

He dreamed
of lemon-scented women
whose words and kisses
corroded his skin.
He dreamed
of raw-edged tins and endings.

So, he took to eating Brie for supper
and the angles of his nightmares
were buffered.
He remembered love
without sharpness
and it settled around his body
like fleece.

## A New Pair of Hands in his Life

They will be shaped
like cream Calla Lily buds,
delicate, weightless and tapered,
able to rest on surfaces
without leaving stains or indentations.

The owner of these hands
will be called Cho He or Mi Cha;
a name which denotes
grace and beauty.

Everything she does
with these pretty little hands,
peeling ginger, beating Pa Jun batter,
fastening buttons
or chopping cabbage for Kim-chi,
will be a genteel cabaret
that he will never tire of watching.

These hands will know
how to coax calm,
reason and charm
into every situation.
They will never be blunt,
clumsy or blatant.
When she laughs
they will hover on her lips
like Brimstone butterflies.
When she yawns
they will flutter
over her mouth
like prayer flags.

Her hands will know
how to be still
and never feel the need
to grab and cling
and, unlike mine,
he'll be happy
to let these hands
weave him
into her life.

### Rendezvous

Don't worry,
it's not too late.
I'll shrink
those vast,
awful nights
you gave me
in the hot-wash,
bring them out
warm, small
and harmless
as dolls' dresses.

I'll empty
my sagging purse
of coins,
stuff it with forgetfulness,
gypsy charms
and street maps.
And I'll wear
my mermaid frock,
meet you
on the horizon
with fish scales
glittering
in my hair.

## About the Author

**Gaia Holmes** is a Yorkshire poet whose work digs beneath the surface of mundane, urban life to reveal a remarkable seam of exoticism. Her debut poetry collection, *Dr James Graham's Celestial Bed* was published in 2006 by Comma Press. This is her second collection.

ALSO AVAILABLE FROM THIS AUTHOR:

# Dr James Graham's Celestial Bed

Gaia Holmes

£7.95
ISBN: 978-0954828080

Praise for Gaia's first collection:

*'Sassy and streetwise, dark and blue, these are poems that are high on words; full of rich imaginings and dislocated love affairs, peopled with ordinary folk made exotic and with the strange made true. Read them.'*
–Amanda Dalton

*'These poems are made from intense sensual experience, bursting with colours, flavours and textures. Gaia Holmes has an eye for the strangeness of things, from "fat lenses of jellyfish / packed in jigsaws of ice" to the sounds and smells of the steelworks, where "metal shrieks as it softens and throbs / under the core of heat".'*
– Jean Sprackland

*'There's something in these poems that I can only call "detailed intimacy" and "closely-worked humanity"; the language is inclusive but still challenging and draws me in to reading after reading. A splendid collection that will grow on you.'*
– Ian McMillan